For all my friends
but especially for Carys, David, and Helen,
who were there at the birth

To find out more about
Simon James and his books, visit
simonjamesbooks.com

Copyright © 2004 by Simon James

First U.S. edition 2004

Library of Congress Cataloging-in-Publication Data is available.

Library of Congress Catalog Card Number 2003065528

ISBN 0-7636-2507-8

2 4 6 8 10 9 7 5 3 1

Printed in China

This book was typeset in Cochin.
The illustrations were done in watercolor and ink.

Candlewick Press
2067 Massachusetts Avenue
Cambridge, Massachusetts 02140

visit us at www.candlewick.com

Baby ✳ Brains

Simon James

CANDLEWICK PRESS
CAMBRIDGE, MASSACHUSETTS

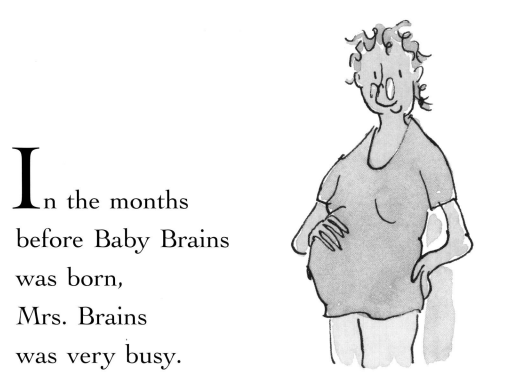

In the months
before Baby Brains
was born,
Mrs. Brains
was very busy.

She read out loud every night to the baby inside her tummy.

She played music and languages on headphones
to her baby during the day.
Mr. and Mrs. Brains wanted to make sure their baby
was going to be very smart.

They even turned up the television when the news came on.

Mr. and Mrs. Brains were very excited when
their baby was born. It was a boy.
"Our very own Baby Brains," said Mr. Brains proudly.

When they brought him home from the hospital,
Mrs. Brains laid him down in the brand-new crib.
"Sleep tight, Baby Brains," she whispered.

The next morning, Mrs. Brains was on
her way to get breakfast when she heard some
strange noises in the living room.

Mrs. Brains opened the door to see her baby sitting
on the sofa, reading the morning paper.

By afternoon, Baby Brains was fixing the car.
"We certainly have a bright one here!" said Mr. Brains.

That evening, Baby Brains spoke his first words. . . .

"I'd like to go to school tomorrow," he said.

The next day, Baby Brains visited the local school.
He sat down with the children and answered all
the questions. The children were amazed.

At the end of the afternoon, the teacher thanked Baby Brains. "I don't think I've ever learned so much in one day," she said.

On the way home, Baby Brains said he wanted to go to college and study medicine.

After just two weeks, Baby Brains began working
as a doctor at the local hospital. He was very popular
with all the staff and patients.

Word soon spread about the extraordinary Baby Brains.
Everyone wanted to meet him.

One night, some
space scientists
called.
They asked if
Baby Brains
would like to
help with their
next space mission.

The following day, Mr. and Mrs. Brains and
their baby traveled to the space center.
After training hard over the weekend . . .

Baby Brains waved goodbye to Mr. and Mrs. Brains
and blasted off into outer space.

Everyone in the world held their breath as they watched
Baby Brains take his first space walk.
"Tell us how you feel on this special occasion,"
radioed Ground Control.

Baby Brains looked up at the vast starlit sky above him.

He looked down at the vast starlit sky below him.

He looked at the whole world in front of him and mumbled something.

"We can't quite hear you," radioed Ground Control.
"Could you repeat that?"

"I want my mommy!"

wailed Baby Brains.

"That's enough!" Mrs. Brains yelled to the
space controller.
"Bring my baby home right now!"

Baby Brains was flown home as quickly as possible. He felt very embarrassed as he stepped down from the hatch.

But, through the crowd of photographers and cameramen,
Mrs. Brains came running.

"Our beautiful little baby," sighed Mrs. Brains
as she lifted him high into the air.
"Our brave little baby," said Mr. Brains.
"Can we go home?" asked Baby Brains.

At home,
Mrs. Brains gave
Baby Brains
a warm bath,

which made him
feel a lot better.

Mr. Brains tickled
him, which made
him laugh.

And Mrs. Brains sang Baby Brains to sleep.
Then they gently laid him down in the brand-new crib.

It was good to have their baby home again.
"Our very own Baby Brains," whispered Mrs. Brains.

From that day on, Baby Brains
spent most of his time at
home, doing the things that
most babies do.
Except, that is, on weekends . . .

when he still liked to
help out at the local hospital.